Quackers and Cheese

Samantha Patterson

ISBN:
Paper Back: 978-1-952320-79-8
Hard Back: 978-1-952320-80-4

Quackers and Cheese

Yorkshire Publishing
4613 E. 91st St,
Tulsa, OK 74137
www.YorkshirePublishing.com
918.394.2665

Printed in the USA

For all my littles—The story starts with you!
Jacob, Ethan, Bralynn, Axton,
River, Maesleigh, Maxxden, Hollis,
Kenny, Eason, Archer, and David

My name is Quackers and his is Cheese.
An unlikely pair, if you please.

We found each other through
misfortune and luck.
A fire in the forest made us run and duck.

I wandered for hours when
the fire was out.
Sad and alone, I began to shout.

I was looking for my Mommy
and my Daddy too.
I didn't know what I was to do.

I wondered up on an old camp site.
A raccoon was there, waiting for night.

I saw him moving slowly from
one basket to another.
He was opening each one,
looking for his brother.

I watched for some time and
saw the tears begin to fall.
He couldn't find anyone
that he tried to call.

He was lost and scared, just like me.
But he was different, that I could see.

He became hungry and began to search.
He climbed up the big old Birch.

He came back down and
looked once more.
There was no food on the forest floor.

He went back to the basket,
looking for lunch.
Out he popped and began to munch.

He looked around and
found me at his back.
I began to quack, quack, quack.

He reached in the basket and
brought out some crackers,

Ready to throw them at his attacker.
"Quack! Quack! Quacker!".
I just need a "snacker"

He found a piece of cheese.
"Can I have a bite, please?"

We sat down together, no longer alone.
But missing our family and our home .

I looked at him and he looked at me.
Best of friends we decided to be.

He doesn't have a bill or even any feathers.
But he has a way of dealing
with life's weathers.

This is how we met, starting
stories such as these.

This is the beginning of
Quackers and Cheese.

CPSIA information can be obtained
at www.ICGtesting.com
Printed in the USA
LVHW072009051120
670549LV00018B/49